LOST AUGUST

LOST AUGUST

POEMS

ESTA SPALDING

Published in 1999 by
House of Anansi Press Limited
34 Lesmill Road, Toronto, ON
Canada M3B 2T6
Tel. (416) 445-3333
Fax (416) 445-5967
www.anansi.ca

Distributed in Canada by
General Distribution Services Inc.
325 Humber College Blvd., Etobicoke, ON
Canada M9W 7C3
Tel. (416) 213-1919
Fax (416) 213-1917
E-mail Customer.Service@ccmailgw.genpub.com

03 02 01 00 99   1 2 3 4 5

CANADIAN CATALOGUING IN PUBLICATION DATA
Spalding, Esta
Lost August
Poems.
ISBN 0-88784-635-1
I. Title

PS8587.P214L67 1999 C811'.54 C98-933057–5
PR9199.3S62L67 1999

Cover design: Angel Guerra
Printed and bound in Canada
Typesetting: ECW Type & Art, Oakville

*House of Anansi Press gratefully acknowledges the Canada Council
for the Arts, the Government of Canada through the Book
Publishing Industry Development Program (BPIDP), and the
Ontario Arts Council for their support of our publishing program.*

for Philip Spalding
for Gillian & Douglas
& in memory of Lin Coburn

CONTENTS

August — or was it August?

Everywhere the river &

Apart, I Send You News of Lions

Each moment is twinned,
you said, each apart from each.
If you listen, there are two
rivers. We inhabit nothing
so much as loss.

You studied frescoes
where gold-leaf palaces
have fallen away.
There, a warrior rides
into absence, province
of the heart.

In another, a grieving father
sends four lions to four
corners to bring his daughter home.
When she comes
she holds out her heart
to him —
there's not gold enough
in any kingdom
to weigh that heart against.

Here, rain's scrubbed clean
the poppy's long-celled stems
each heavy with the lion-
hearted blossom.
Four petals, one for each direction.

I see you everywhere I can.

Listen, I tried to leave
a message. *Will you see
how you are wrong: both
rivers, the same river
in us, the very one.*

Aperture

Those summers at Kamakai'po
our tents pimpled the beach, but
we four lay half-buried in sand
under a zoo of stars, naming the animals
as we fought sleep.

In the morning our bodies
were circled with crab tracks
like constellations.

Kamakai'po, cove where the road widens
between *kiawe* trees, coral reef juts
over the horizon. Where waves
trapped in the reef-neck swell the beach.
'Opihi hooded in their shells
nurse on volcanic rock.

Did we watch sun rise & set
into the same sea
from that beach?
I remember it that way
as I recall the morning light
was distilled by bees
who worked in darkness, stealing
sour milk, kerosene, & axle grease.

The bees, small factories
made the wretched sweet.

⌒

In our father's photographs
from those summers
there is nothing
of weight. Light flickers from
the dullest rock
as if he saw all objects levitating,
as if his camera held for a moment
what would dissolve.

He shot thousands of rocks,
sometimes at arm's length, sometimes
from airplanes. They all look the same,
still life.

In a photograph of the *heiau*, light beams
shoot upward, a smear of lime & rose. I want

stones to hold down the edges
of the frame but they waver
developing before the eye
so his photographs tell certain lies.

꙳

Always bent on work, even at Kamakai'po
our father did something with his hands.

Unsatisfied as the sea,
he spent our childhoods breaking rock.
A hard black stone in his palm pecked
at the grey stone, someday
it would be an implement to pound taro root.

Belly thrust, his trunk sunk in sand,
he ground the stone till flecks of light

powdered his legs.
Held to the sun,
our father would burn.

If I pound long enough, he said, *I'll bury us.*
We, intent on other stories, busy growing new
skins, ran back toward the sea, hurling
our maroon bodies into wave face.
Underwater, we waited for the sun to drop
a pearl into cold hands.

⌒

Our father knew secrets.
Tapping stones, whispering chants,
he sang the hidden names of places.
No compass but his voice, the songs,
he found things: the grave
of a mother & child. Two bodies wrapped
in paper skin — as dead as we were alive.

He found *heiaus*, homesites, sacred
stones. He found sources for the names.

At night, by lantern eye, he mapped these sites
& those things we found with our songs:
deer antlers, shell casings,
adze heads, *ulumaika*.

Trying to make magic ourselves,
we four conferred under vigilant
stars. A bowl dug in sand, filled with cow dung
was a trick to make fire. We poked

the flame with *kiawe* branches, then raced
down the beach writing against the night
words that lingered — our names brief as light.

Sark told the best stories: night marchers
who roamed looking for children. The *menehunes*
would wreck your car if you carried pork at night.
Cricket Man stole your voice when his silver
hands touched your throat.

Never step on the stone that marks the *Ali'i*'s grave
on that stone no moss would grow.
Never play drums in the mountains.

Wild with fear
& pleasure we vowed to stay awake.
In the morning we found
sleep had stolen us again.

⁀

Water's memory,
the fat toad in the pool of rain
deep in the desert.

We walked all day, our father's broad
body before us. His shirt pulled off, padding his
shoulder where the tripod rested.
His crack just lifting over his belt, he hauled himself,
camera, tripod, case
rock by rock
up the parched lip of the valley.
The whole island was dirt, red as a woman's blood.

We were going to find *Kaana, Ka Hula Piko*,
birthplace of hula where the gods taught
a woman to dance. It was a place you had to feel.

Ignoring thirst, I searched the red mud
for deer antlers. Each year the deer grew
another rack with one more point — the deer's body
kept track. Knowledge locked in the forehead.
Imagine scampering over rocks
carrying that. Imagine the itch.

He forged on. The tripod, dipping forward,
was an anvil beating the still metal
air. We shuffled twice for each stride of his,
a skittish herd, moving up a dry riverbed.

No one complained. We measured tired legs
against acres of loneliness.

So dry I wanted to crack, I was finally going
to say something brave, to get his attention
& see his face — I had stared all day at his back,
the calligraphy of his spine, each vertebra a stone
pressing through his skin.

My breasts, hard stones thrown in
the pool of my chest, ached in circles.

I was going to screech as loud as the branches
tearing open the sky, when
the toad appeared.

That toad in the riverbed
that had dreamt for months of water
dove across the *kiawe*, a rumour

of something else.
We followed it into the brush
till arms & legs were scratched to knife wounds.

Suddenly the pool.
Up to our necks, we soaked & gulped,
pressed water through our teeth, opened
our eyes to drink.
The careless toad between our kelp legs.

Though the water would dry to filth
on my skin, I lifted my shirt: pure ablution.

After that day, every man was measured against
the wound my father made

against that gift.

⌐

Was the last summer a sum of the others
or maybe a trick to make sense?

We rode on the hood of the Jeep, singing
the names he had taught us.
Moloka'i nui a Hina.

My father handed down his Nikon
along with formulas:
never shoot for more than 1/200th,
high aperture, low f-stop.

I photographed in daylight. My camera
always set on the same exposure.

That summer Sage uncovered a trunk
of sticky yellow packages — parachutes?
We opened them, imagining holding hands & falling
together into the rushing map of land.

My father found us. *Plastic explosives*, he said.
The picture shifted: we were charred
blown separated. We might ignite.
The long ropes I had believed would hold us
were wicks. The sun, suddenly too bright.

⌒

The last morning
Sage stepped on a beehive.
The Jeep got a flat.
What else could happen?

We hit a stone & Sark slipped,
ocean-wet, from the hood,
beneath the tires.

Behind us, on the road
what was left of him
screamed to break the shriek of *kiawe*.
Blood sheeting out of him
the colour of that rich dirt.

Time, light, the terrible pulse
of circumstance
fell into place.
The earth charting its course,
sky still overhead.
We aged in an instant.

Though Sark lived, my father
never photographed again.
He said he had been cursed
for his camera work, for ignoring
the gravity of things.

After We Met

Come, you said, holding your hand
out to me, *come*
& I remember Summer,
the old horse no one
could ride till one lost day
when the stable was
empty. I had a handful of smashed
strawberries, clutched
all the way across the field.
Summer came
to the wooden gate where I hung
over the top plank
& he blew wet breath onto
my sweetened hand. Then
he took those berries gently
into his famous, terrible mouth.

No, he did not let me sit on his back.
Where would we have gone, anyway,
a piss-yellow horse stuck behind
a gate & an uncombed
girl without a key?
But I tell you, he may as well have,
we both knew.
I swear, the way he looked
at me without blinking & moved
his lips, kind, wet, across
the lines of my palm that
even then said something about you.
For fifteen minutes,
I sat in the straw of his stall
quietly breathing, watching his

quiet breathing
his tail seldom flicking
at the endless traffic of flies.

What they tell you isn't always true.

Come, you said, quietly breathing.
I didn't scare you.
I didn't scare you.

Archaeology

It requires a scientist's precision to move
over you, excavating
river bed
gully, plates that shift
leaving fragments extruded —
fossil, petrified
shell, a chipped stone adze
as when I touched your tailbone
& you remembered in a fleeting shadow
of a dream your first dead.

That girl in your fifth-grade class
dead, car whirling into
the ravine — a fall day, wet crimson leaves
that time of year, the word *fall*
came to mean skidding
over the edges of things.
When I touched you,
you recalled praying
for her on your knees,
as if you were the one chosen
to forge her path, cleaving to heaven
you took her into your
body, slick leaves, cells
of black concrete, swallowed with the swollen prayer,
river prayer, the road over the edge
you would follow, pack your own vivid body
into the absence behind the car,
you would take her
death into you
something solid, lodged compactly
at the base of the spine,

an artifact any careful lover
might dust with precise brushes
& seeing its amber, its red
restore the burnished coins
that weight the eyes of the dead.

Canoe

That moment before sleep steals
him, that moment he is in her
arms, face pressed between collarbone
& neck, a moment she holds
his still breathing form — he turns
into a river.

She presses her fingers into
his skin & glides out as a canoe
will just part the surface that closes
over its stern.

She will dive under
water like sleep
holding her breath, feeling the river's pressing
embrace, lie on her back, stare at
the stars' fingerprints.

Each night she marries the river, a bride
promising herself to the one
beside her — each touch is a current
that carries her away
from herself,

then back again,
the way she loses herself
& is found in new arms.

An Apology

Each day you wake first
put the coffee on
then whistling to our deaf dog
lunge into morning.
The two of you
noses to the wind
cross the crooked sidewalk
the one busy street — empty
at that hour — & down to the water.
(Blown across ocean
the clouds arrive above you
full of desire.)
                You will come home —
the dog already campaigning
for breakfast — & only then
wake me to tell me
what you know —
how many clouds hung on
this morning's mountains.

(Sometimes when I think of how
much you carry on your narrow
beautiful back my heart will ache.)

For the first time
this morning I left you
sleeping & rose to cross
the floorboards.
But looking down at you
I could not embark.
I had sailed all night
to arrive. Your face pressed

to the pillow
your tightly curled fists.
How could I come to the mountain
& not open my mouth — let
the rain fall where it will?
How could I not wake you, tell you
what I just then knew?

November 3:57

Beyond the glass a seal-grey sea
mountains & pink flicker
the upholsterer's neon light
whoosh tik tik the upstairs
neighbour's drying his jeans
again *whoosh* & two metal rivets hit
the cylinder *tik tik* the confession
of lint then pink off again
on again & the 4th
Avenue bus whirrs its
nervous circuit round the corner
at Alma *whoosh tik tik* three hours ago a twin-
engine Cessna lifted off the runway beside
the migrant camp bearing crates of pears
some picked by a man whose son lies in bed
his leg in a cast
the green-stick bones twisted
he thinks of his son as he
picks the last pear hearing the quiet pop
the pear makes pulling off the branch that springs
from his hand
that pear on the plane
just now in frame
above ghost mountains above
buses & pinks
& *whoosh* like a river the boy once played in
calling out for his father as twin dragonflies
light *tik tik* on the water

Another Love Poem in Which the Neighbours Complain

The kettle elemental
a fire under it
geese outside
the window though it's winter
& the city it's our heat
that keeps them circling
their wings make a flap to shake
foundations of the poem in which
the neighbours complain

Wings & kettle coming quickly
to a boil we are on knees
having fallen forward into
arms the neighbours banging
against our walls
knocked the picture from its
frame the kettle nearly singing
fogs every window
a way of saying the room
is small like my hands on
your shoulders & the fists
of the neighbours *keep it down*

On the floor beside us the picture
(our daughter   a yellow dress)
already two cups on saucers wait
but we are more occupied
the question there between us
who will turn off the element
its tiara of fire?
My hands still on your shoulders
yours on mine
the neighbours taking matters

into their own hands call the landlord
those geese scissoring
horizon cut sea from sky
& the light that floods from two bodies
each shadow to the other o the steam
whistling like a bullet when love's struck
& the neighbours should complain
we're putting holes in the walls

Passing Through

I am writing to tell you how it was
while you were with Anne
digging clams.

The peacock under the bower, sheep
in the paddock, golden eagle.
You & Anne gone with a bucket.
Three dogs, eleven legs between them.
Nothing can disturb the afternoon
except its own passing through.
The wind.
I wait out the chill
between bursts of sun.

Were you here, I would ask:
if the light falling now left the sun
a million years ago, why
does it disappear when
that sun dips behind a cloud?

I am writing to say I told you so.
Told you we would
eat the clams. The eagle
& the peacock would
have it out.
Later we would make love.
The child my parents did not
expect that night
on the Mexico border
& the child your mother won
after they scraped her
clean, those children giving themselves
to each other, to desire,
the fall toward something.

I know — as the shadow of a jet
passes between me & the
page — by the time the bucket's
full, by the time I
read this to you, the afternoon will be
eaten. Only our atoms still,
falling, only the peacock's foolish call.

Lately Fallen

It was true what they'd told us
about desire: the still
woods, heavy with imperfect
trees, the lately fallen
needles soft beneath our feet
the impromptu walk
& what they'd described about our hands
the hinge of two wings, their long
feathers touching at the point
above the animal
centre, those wings
stroking to rise
for a moment
desire above every
thing even
the truth: what they'd
said: those hinges
held a door,
opened once,
open to another, another.

Politics

Tanks rolled into Tiananmen Square as you leaned over to
me, across the Formica table of Bar Le Sportif. How grass
green your eyes were — I had just learned your name, also
Green, I was laughing, on-screen soldiers croaked through
loudspeakers at the students rooted there.

We talked politics. I couldn't look away from you —
long brown throat tipped back, the slender glass in your left
hand, deep brown liquid, like a woman's blood, sliding into
your mouth. I wanted to. So angry about those men your lips,
eyes brightened as you spoke of them. On my napkin you
wrote, *André Malraux, La Condition humaine.*

These were my politics: you across the table, a bend in
your elbow, a dimple at the wrist as if you had been kissed
(who was it?) your long fingers on the pen, curl of each letter
like soft hairs between the legs — over my head, supple
bodies before the tanks.

No East or West

Above the bay, an F-14 leaves
a worshipful scar in its wake.
Walking beside the air
force base, beside the sea,
I tilt my face away from the waves,
suck in breath as the silhouette
of the twilight fighter intersects
the black figure of a pelican.
It hovers, patient
for a mercurial scale-glint
then dives as the tail
lights disappear in constellations
of satellites.

What could be more marvellous
than the message exhaust
leaves, orange above the blue cedars?

On the kelp-littered beach
the vanished
footprints of those who first
stumbled from the scrub-dusty hills,
gasping at the blessing of so much water.

Such fragile beings, they were buried
a thousand years before this moment
spent between the dying sea
& the underpass where stoplights change
with mystical regularity.

Pity those innocent of the green going
who die before
this end of the world.

The Dog's Prescription

What he needs, my step-
mother says, *is a good*
whack between the eyes.

Days when coffee's brewed
on yesterday's grounds or car's
stalled in front of the laundromat
where comfort shrinks
with each loonie

& the little girl next
door peeks through the rotten
fence, saying, *is he what you'd call*
your baby?

those days, you'll swallow
whatever it takes
to still the heart's
dogged worm.

May, Pregnant

Whose fault is it
the dogwoods bloom, spilling
cups of pink milk onto
the swollen asphalt.
We can't take them back.

Sprung from berths,
the ships with full-
bellied sails
move in one direction.
The wind's a decision
they didn't make.
Mother, May I?

Last night I wanted
to wake you,
I wanted to tell you
what I know: once
it flowers the swarm
comes, hungry.

It's death
who breathes the first
air into our lungs.

Salad Days

I was certain it was the beginning
of the end. We were taking vitamins.

With coffee, I popped folic acid
on the off chance I was
pregnant. I was smoking.
I was chain-smoking. Even the
prime minister admitted to
global warming.
We knew that counted.
Just the same junk cooked
in the air & I
smoked. Nothing was happening
fast enough to indicate.

      Missiles were turned
on countries with unacceptable
behaviour. Some sulked, some pouted.
      Missiles were turned
on countries intending to build
missiles.
      They were pointed at us.

At night we made room on the bed
for the dog. Not from generosity — he
would stand at the foot & bark.
Like everyone else, he wanted his.

We held each other close, mostly
to make room for the dog.
Furthermore, he tracked
sand into the bed & farted
more than we did.

Sometimes at night
sand would trouble the
skin on my back & I
would wake aching
with clear knowledge:
we were all three
miraculously breathing.

Above us, the satellites gathered
in formation.

We waited for the missiles.
The water rose around us.

One morning when you woke
you said you'd been driving with your
brother to the top of a hill.
Breathing sun-warmed air, the two of you
looked out on a quilt of fields.
As a boy he never liked vegetables,
but in the dream he took you to
an all-you-can-eat salad bar.
You ate together as if he were alive.

In my dream
I considered dyeing
my hair.

How are you, love? you asked that morning.

I wouldn't change an atom.

Marriage in the Last Days

If what the body knows — that in leaping off
it continues to fall
cascade heel
over head
if what the body knows
is true — the swoop
not the end
in net or cement
in the arms of the attendants
if the body's knowledge is without
hesitation (the mind that films
it framing lines between instances
the mind adding time to body-continuous
fear arising dragon-headed
in what will be
the mind's will gulping the future
arriving too soon
at the bone-shocked end
not poised — mid-leap —
with dear physiology
not lingering present
& accounted for.

Last night the dream of blue fighters
lifting off to the final raising
to the event that would undo events
or stitch them to time
the fighter planes
of the mind constituting the end
of mind-bound bodies
time compacted to a wafer
no more end
over end just
the last station
of the stopped unsorry world.

This, a dream of the mind
not body (heavy on its sheets unspoiled
as the eucalyptus outside the window
pageless pageless drinking
the green worm-rich soil
still making a living
denying an end.

Last night the body
numb to the mind-blue silhouettes
lifted itself on weak wrists
& moved over the other body in the bed, saying, *Here
is an edge & I will have it, Here
is something to give wholly
myself, Here is a fire to feed, no not a
fire, Here, an edge, Yes, Here is air, marry me.*

Each girl, the one

for girlfriends

Before the Worm

Before the worm who ate a hole
in night, before regret we sat
on the back stoop spitting cherry seeds.

Spitting for accuracy,
on the honour system,
into the dark.
Spitting true & for keeps
at that god of knocked-out teeth.

Nothing to wish for
but spit & listen —
pong on concrete.

The seeds prayed *seduce*
me to air that whispered
summer's hidden somewhere.
We took from each other
hungry as nostalgia.
                    (She was the eye of
                    the bird that moved
                    into my skin.)
We shrugged off everything else
for those out on stoops
losing themselves.
                    (She sliced between her fingers
                    took it to my mouth —
                    I tasted blood, the last seed tossed
                    into blind night, tossed before
                    the worm sprouted there.)

Scar

I hung upon your face that night, the only night, hooked
upon the half-moon & the bladed stars. You were telling me
about the accident & why your back was always to the wall,
that night, the only night you were straight with me, I
couldn't help but wrap your breath around my neck to keep
warm, snow etherizing the city — we were immune, though
later what you told me would fever.

We walked six miles that night (I counted them later, taking
the same steps). I don't remember anything, but I held what I
could: the other side of your face laughing when you tipped
your hat to that girl crouched on the glazed sidewalk,
fingering cracks. I bent down & found a tooth from a deer,
somehow loose between the gold towers & highways.

I wear that scarf still.
Don't you dare think what's between us is nothing.

Or the Eye

Speaking of fathers
        their silence or absence
we walk the trail between cliff
        & sea barely looking at who
passes or the eye of the heron moving
        into shadows beneath silver water their
silence or absence flicker
        of a body beneath the silver
flicker of dark inside the smudge of the heron's own
        shadow we are trying to say something
but the words go as soon as we have spoken
        what remains of the rain
straining through red cliffs to the sea
        our faces wet though our hoods are up
the heron hunting still the path
        that worms between trees
last year when we were here
        three men knee-deep in mud
digging for the missing boy —

Winter Orchid

This winter
two doors — one
of them your face,
the way you will turn
to me, your eyes coming
into the light,
saying: abandon
the other door, abandon
your only life.

You promised me
your arms —

In truth you said no
such thing. In truth
it was your
hand on the table where
my head rested — it was
your breath
becoming air —

The last time I
touched your breast
it was to know the orchid
of cancer there.

When the Box Arrived

Express mail from Honolulu (all
those vowels in the postman's mouth
were cloud puffs in cold air).
Below the tissue:
                strands & strands
of ginger blossoms, delicate as the thread that held
them. An equator's fragile snow.
A box transporting
the reflection of moon in water, the moment
when branches bend, the sky
between azure & storm.
Pacific air filled the stale apartment:
four of us ankle-deep in mud
beside the river's skirt. Mosquitoes
big as guavas, blood & insect guts under our nails,
water pooled in palm frond saucers, our eyes
drunk on hibiscus, bougainvillea, bird
of paradise. Up river, carrying Japanese shears
to snip ginger that would wither
before we reached home.

Rainy Day List

Sage's Favourite Surfing Waves:
Bowls, Rock Piles, In-Betweens, Canoes,
Queens, Publics, Uluwatus, No Place,
Old Mans, Rice Bowls, Zeros, Tongs, Winch,
Radicals, Graveyards, Sleepy Hollows,
Lighthouse, Cliffs, Halemanus, Cow Piss Corner,
Hunakais, Razors, Bones, Tosh Kanes, Oki Choo Choo,
Secrets, Toes, Snips, Blue Hole, Turtles,
Finger, Kevorkians, Five O'Clocks, Mental Oafs,
Makapu'u, Palava Point, Cockroach Bay,
Magnums, No Can Tells, Blackouts,
Way the Fucks, Pyramid Rock, Batu Lefts,
Sugar Mills, Shittys, Razorbacks, Crouching Lion,
Pounders, Gutters, Bong Water Reef,
Revelations, Indicators, Velzy Land,
Sunset Point, Pupukea, Ehukai, Pipeline,
Backdoor Pipeline, Keiki, Rubber Duckies,
Waimea, The Pouch, Alligator Rock, Laniakea, Himalayas,
Icons, Avalanche, Speed Reef, Silver Channel,
Yokohamas, Pray for Sex, Makuas, Free Hawai'i,
Makaha, Claus Meyers, Green Lantern, Uliawa,
Sewers, Maile Point, Reef Runway, Point Panic,
Kewalos, Bomburros, Bowls

Getting Back

Take the long way round
the island to that cove pocketed
between hill & sea. Lanikai.
One path into, one path out
rising to the point that hangs over reef.
                                    Pull over
beside the Chevy junkers, old Mustangs
dangling dice from their mirrors,
brilliant feathers, hash pipes.
When you were 10 you were afraid
of these men whose engines
backfired drag racing past your window
each night. In daylight
you watched through tinted glass
as they slid needles in or tipped
bottles back, the butt
of an oily gun between the thighs.

Now you meet their glazed eyes.

Tilt your head back to see perched
above rocks the Bird Woman's house.
She lives alone, sleeps on a bed
carved from volcanic cliff.
                                    Kick up
your kickstand, pedal the last few rounds.
Coast down into Lanikai.

The air shifts. Salt so heavy you taste it.
Yards filled with coconut trees, stubble of itchy
grass & dried coconuts cracked
by tiny trees that stab up
from dark insides.

Rose & Mary's place
where the tire hangs from a rope
slung over the banyan tree, its roots
above ground. Alani's
where you spent the afternoon
in the castaway cardboard box
that brought her mother's new fridge.
Alani, Keithi Jones, & you taking turns
taking off your shorts. Nobody knew
but you emerged wise. All 3 of you vowed
to jump on Alani's bed 1000 times & you did it too.
You had never believed 1000 was a number
to be counted to. You flew up on 999
like 3 stray planets
came down & then went
up again. Somewhere between 999 & 1000
you decided life wasn't going to scare you.

Keep pedalling, if your old legs are tired, stand
on the pedals one at a time —
it takes 105 to roll you home.
It's just as you expected: 2 stories tall
the highest house in the neighbourhood.
The roof still droops down, the steps
to the second floor are on the outside, the old red van
is pulled up in the drive. Mynah birds bitch
in the hibiscus, their bright yellow eyes
target you. You have arrived.
You will step back inside, hear
the clatter of Rob the silversmith who lived
downstairs, who melted a bracelet
around your arm when you turned 10
& gave you a toke from his pipe.
(15 years ago someone shot him in the head.)
You'll take the stairs 2 at a time & inside

all those fish you overfed, their silver bellies
rising to the surface, will be alive.
Your mother will be soaking soybeans & listening
to the Beatles. The kettle singing to the glass
window slates, dusty in afternoon sun.
Throw down your bike. But before
you go in: close your eyes, count
as high as you can.

Roommate

When we met again on the subway platform
it was five o'clock in the middle of the city
where we had been children.
I had just flown in
afraid of America
& Chicago & the South Side.
I had forgotten
how to be always-at-war.
The car was full of
faces scarred with grease.
You had a briefcase
a new pleated skirt.
Across from us
a man wearing shorts,
his body thick with tattoos.
They seemed to rise from his muscles.
Blue-black dragons
hearts, skulls, fists, a snake around his neck.

We walked to the restaurant
across a puddled street, under
the oily ribs of the L tracks.

You said, tell me about your life.
You first, I said.
(Did we even know each other?)
You said, strike. You used words
I once mouthed: labour, solidarity, human rights.
You told how you stood
on the picket lines, how in court
you worked so they could work.
They teach me how to live, you said.

Your hands moving intricately
like the paws of a field
mouse, your delicate chopsticks
picking up rice
a few grains
at a time.

I thought how we lay awake
in our twin beds
under ruffled sheets,
our dorm room deep in the grid of that city
we whispered into dark air promises —
all the things we would do.
In the morning, I forgot them.
In you, they rose up
indelible on your skin.

Recipe

At first she wouldn't eat beef.
She lived with the living meat, swam in
the lame eyes of veal. Then
neither chicken nor fish,
nothing with a face.
She took no lover
who ate it, no tainted kiss. Now she won't
read anything written by one carnivorous:
images brewed on flesh, on bone.

I wanted to write for her something
with a vegetable base — I'm finding my mind has
changed, branching, it drinks
sometimes entirely brightness —

Tadpole Dreams

Falling asleep in a narrow room.
Beyond one wall, a chorus of August frogs, beyond
the other you watch a Chinese opera.

Will the daughter betray her father,
find the legs, feet to leave the marsh?
Will she open her throat to the 'flying-up moon,'
that cup of milk left on the stoop
outside my window?

The Apprentice

What he stole from them wasn't theirs
entirely, was the loose gold
coin, the stray cat that wandered
in from red trees. He stole
their dreams: weddings they'd never
attended, frozen fountains, fist-sized
pyramids. He stole too many snakes,
daggers, graves. Countless women on top of men
men above women & the secret women
with women, men with men. Dozens
of Monets & not enough Rembrandts
for his taste. He stole their blue
periods, insects hissing
in foreign languages, an unknown light
house that held childhood,
top hats, a yellow feather in a sister's hand, train
whistles, grandmothers on ice
skates, a father lifting his daughter's
veil, the twangling
instrument of rain. All slipped
from the dreamers' heads,
wallets from pockets, rings
off stunned fingers, yanked chains, a jewelled chest
pried open.

Nothing he took from them mattered —
but it was everything, the edge
of the known world.

His victims slept so empty
they were pale, morbid, silent. Woke
without weeping, complaint,
or colours. With only the impression
a hat, a cuff, a sole was vanishing.

Notes on a Poem about Juls

Possible opening — shared fear
of airplanes? Hairbrushes or
that checkout guy, Rod, at liquor control?
Maybe favours you've done her: like time
gruesome medical student
who gave Juls Pap smear
asked for her phone number —
she gave him yours.
Numerous double dates she pretended
not to want dessert, but reached cross table
ate foam from your cappuccino
with her spoon.

Jewels.

A stanza demanding return of
first-edition *Amazons*.

Ask to borrow
her new red boots.
Ask in a way she can't refuse.

Divine

Even the grapes aren't wicked enough
to tell — they lack discretion
being sisters in crime
having chosen
the bottle with the viper coiled in it
eau-de-vie *de* snake venom —
even the grapes can't
say though they were in it
from the beginning like a hurricane
bickering over just how much sweetness
& where to put it blowing
out the candle in another hotel room
that summer we were so beautiful
we kept shattering porcelain.

For months every time I looked in the mirror
I saw you.

There was marble & the muscled
canvases — gelato stained our lips.
How much life can skin hold? We blistered
bruised as grapes begging
to be wine. There should have been
more boats in it
fewer men. We were spoiled
on the vine hanging
out of train windows standing up on our
pedals winging curse or praise
in our own romance
language *Raccrochez la ligne! Dové
formaggio?* Our tongues knew things
even the grapes don't know
snug in their barrels
though years from now we will unstop
those missing girls.

Once Rapture

The summer of the factory
fire we grew wild.

Avoid your gardens, the radio
said, but

who listened? Our ears trowelled
wet ground

we slipped down gutters, fingered man-
hole covers.

There was something in the ash
that came

plummeting, grey bodies of
the doves

something toxic, your tongue
going down

my back & our knack
for lying

side by side beneath
rumbling tracks.

Put your mouth where
my mouth

is, you said, *put your*
honey, money.

The fire, rapture, we drank
& drank.

⌐⌐

The vegetables grow in clean
rows now.

Factory's rebuilt. Train's
rusted still.

I didn't — it's true — but I
meant to,

I meant to, when I find you, I'll
tell you,

I didn't, but I
meant to.

Any fool can see
you're dead,

but in a
certain light,

once rapture, I
catch you

smoking a rolled cigarette. *Been years* — in
a certain

voice, I ask for the match
& inhale.

I will drag you back.

A yellow dress

The Anatomy of Freighters

When everything in us stops & the sound of the rain
is the sound of lost names, the freighters moving up the false
water, everything discharging here at the edge of the known
world, all the names told in her voice, the drowned girl who
calls, throat filled with no language, her call more wound
than silence, when everything in us is married
to that lost cry, to damage.

There is the keel, yes, & then there is the known world, real
estate, stock markets, gasoline, crime, the burnished nails
of the woman who adjusts your claim. Your back. There is
the keel or something else, something revealed, an anger. The
keel held under, a spell, unconscious. There is the blood
spilled daily & then, yes, sometimes there is the
unproclaimed joy:
                                   a yellow dress,
you in sleep, holding me steady, a wheel, the rudder moving
away from shoal, a wheel, yes, sometimes the keel holds us on.

I have watched them open jaws & reach into the hold.
What's buried there, the heroin. What comes clean
into the sky, birds
                    reeling through metal struts, the crane's
steel lattice. I have watched them unpack the ship — a priest
receiving confessions. Hollow-hulled & guiltless. I have
seen the birds struggle into dark hold, each with a gold
straw. My eye goes with them, together we make home in it.

Where were you when the rain came & the great ships seized themselves abandoning the harbour? Where were you that afternoon? Ships hugged shore but I nodded in air, a crane. (You hadn't said my name in a week of nights.) Still the blood country. That girl with her cup & coins on the street below my window. Where the clear end? Her wrists, thin as bird shit. O to disappear: the mouth of the cup, the bent currency. The ship empty as sleep asking her to become that dream they dream, a current.

That afternoon, the girl not there. The ships moored still
empty on the glass harbour. The sun, the blind brilliant eyeball.
Her cup, empty too. & her, not there. Her sign: *Change?* Now
streaked with rain. Ink blurred. Same rain that fell on my
roof. Not hers. Not there. Cargo unpacked from that hold.
The birds, *confess, a home in darkness.*

Before then I walked past every afternoon, taking in her yellow dress, yes, her dress, not body. Sometimes the coin from my pocket to her cup. Sometimes the lightened step, as if to say, *enough, enough.* Then the light burned in my window.

I am going to sea. Waiting to sea. Wading. Beside the
freighters, their effortless discharge, keels free, red as this
country.
                    They found her, she was pulled
into the skiff (my eye went with it). Filled to bursting,
blue with names, given, given, mine among them,
she had told me hers, an exchange. She begged
to the keels that hung suspended above her, birds in false sky.

Her cup on the window. You in my bed. Everything that drowns returns to us as cargo, the ones we carry. She, the child we conceive each night. I have not told you her name, but in sleep I beg for the one whose hold this is.

Two Deer

All day long the pieces.

The hawk by roadside, face deep
in the strings of a dog's belly, two deer running beside four
lanes of highway, necks taut as straining ropes, panic cata-
      pulting them forward, shocked eyes,
           murderous hooves.

      The dead man upright
in the cabin of his truck
beside him
his wife's mouth moves, she is saying
bits of things
      he was just here
      he just slumped
hands curled, the tips of her
fingers twitching, holding her coat, she
says, *We were going to Florida*
      We have friends in Florida
eyes wildly pitched.

What falls from us finds
no place
         nothing to hold.

A Yellow Dress

Everywhere the river &
you beside it.

Each girl, the one
who slipped
from our grasp.

Red boots & a
yellow dress, a
yellow dress.

The pattern we laid
out for her. A needle,
a spool of thread.

Before grief, the shape
of grief —

a pattern stitched *by her own hand*
as fate is sometimes
described in old books we have
often read, turning the
page & passing
our eyes over the final
sentence, the leaves
closed, the book
on the floor, cold
sheets to our shoulders
we have sometimes shut out the light.

Bee Verse

Let the bees come then. Let
there be another time & *enough*.
Let this empty cup brim
another cup.

Let the bees come then, let
them gather us. Let there be
another time & *enough, enough.*
Let this empty cup brim
another cup.
Let there be room
& the afternoon
light against skin, let the comb
rest with the child's hairs
in it.

Let the bees come then, let
them gather us. Let there be
another time & *enough, enough.*
Let this empty cup brim
another cup.
Let the bees golden.
Let there be room
to lie in & the afternoon
light against skin, let the comb
rest on the dresser with
the child's hairs still in it.
Let that ordinary room of
ordinary joy, yellow, & the bees
enter this woman, empty.
Again let there ecstasy, your blue
umbrella upturned in the hall, the red
plastic boots, also wet,
a field of glazed blossoms
busy with stumbling
bees, what honeys from the briefest
touch: petal, pollen: what's borne
aloft on spindled legs. Let
curators of wax
galleries ripen hollowness
to flesh. Let them gift
forth as metaphysicians to fill
us till the improbable becomes us
& absence is distilled
till found & belonging
we gather our faces turned to the sun.

From wretched heart
let the bees deliver us.

August

Skin-tight with longing, like dangerous
girls, the tomatoes reel, drunk
from the vine.

The corn, its secret ears
studded like microphones, transmits August
across the field: paranoid crickets, the noise of snakes
between stalks, peeling themselves from
themselves.

I am burdened as the sky,
clouds, upset buckets pour
their varnish onto earth.

Last year you asked if I was
faint *because of the blood*. The tomatoes
bristled in their improbable skins,
eavesdropping.

This is one way to say it.
The girl gone, you left.

& this another.
Last year in August I hung
my head between my knees, looked up
flirting with atmosphere
but you were here
& the sky had no gravity.

Now love falls from me,
walls from a besieged city.
When I move the mountains shrug off
skin, horizon shudders, I wear the moon
a cowbell.

My symptom:
the earth's
constant rotation.

On the surface the sea argues.
The tide pulls water like a cloth
from the table, beached boats, dishes
left standing. Without apology
nature abandons us.
Returns, promiscuous, & slides between
sheets, unspooling the length
of our bodies.

Black wild rabbits beside the lighthouse
at Letite. They disappear before
I am certain I've seen them.
Have they learned this from you?

I read the journal of the boy who starved
to death on the other side of a river
under trees grown so old he would not feed them
to a signal fire. His last entry:
August 12 Beautiful Blueberries!

Everything I say about desire or
hunger is only lip service
in the face of it.

Still there were days I know
your mouth gave that last taste of blue.

When you said you were
leaving
I pictured a tree,
spring, the green
nippled buds

not the fall
when we are banished
from the garden.

Another woman fell
in love with the sea,
land kissed by salt, the skin
at the neck a tidal zone, she rowed
against the escaping tide
fighting to stay afloat.

To find the sea she had to turn her back to it,
stroke.

The sea is a wound
& in loving it
she learned to love what goes missing.

Once the raspberries grew
into our room, swollen as the
brains of insects, I dreamt a
wedding. We could not find our
way up the twisted ramp, out from under
ground, my hair earth-damp.

I woke. A raspberry bush clung to us
sticky as the toes of frogs.
A warning: you carried betrayal
like a mantis
folded to your chest — legs, wings, tongue
would open, knife
the leaves above us.

If I could step into
your skin, my fingers
into your fingers putting on
gloves, my legs, your legs,
a snake zipping
up. If I could look
out of your tired eyeholes
brain of my brain,
I might know
why we failed.
(Once we thought the same
thoughts, felt the same things.)

A heavy cloak, I wear
you, an old black wing
I can't shrug off.

O heart of my heart,
come home. O flesh,
come to me before
the worm, before earth
ate the girl,
before you left without
belongings.

You said, *there are women*
I know whose presence
changes the quality of air.

I am not one of those. The leaves
lift & sigh, the river
keeps saying the unsayable things.
I hesitate to prod the corn from the coals
though I have soaked it in Arctic water.
I stop the knife near the tomato
skin, all summer coiled there.
You are not coming back.

One step is closer
to the fire.

September will fall
with twilight's metal,
                     loose change
from a pocket. Quicker than
an oar can fight water,
I will look up from my feet
catch the leaves red-handed
embracing smoke.

Around me, lost things gather
for an instant
in earth-dark air.

August, an epilogue

One day a woman will walk
through a door
she misplaced.

There's a chill
but she'll twist the coils
till the radiators stir.

There are walls
of planks still
settling on their studs.

She'll take a broom or rinse
the dusty bucket.
Turn mirrors around.
She'll know the faces
in the pictures &
some of them were hers.

She'll find a comb on the sill with
hairs still in it.
Yes, one day it won't make
a difference. She'll head
through the blue fields & drop
the fist of hair
into backwater.

The poppies will nod,
paper heads aflame.

When she spies the ash-grey
nest between shelf &
chimney, she won't disturb it.

There's company in hornet noise.
In the clock's logic. Her own
dull breath.

In darkness she'll push
peas from skins with her thumb
or grease the tumblers
of all four locks.

Next time the boys come
to drag the lake,
she won't confess
to anything.

Acknowledgements

Some of these poems have been published in a slightly different form in *Brick, Carousel, The Malahat Review, The Colorado Review, Prism International, Blues & True Concussions: Six New Toronto Poets* (Anansi, 1996), *Vintage 1998*. My thanks to the editors of those publications.

For her invaluable editorial advice I am indebted to Sharon Thesen. And to Martha Sharpe & Adrienne Leahey at Anansi. For their help with early drafts of the poems, I am grateful to: Michael Redhill, Janice Kulyk Keefer, Miranda Pearson, Marilyn Dumont, Kate Braid, Shauna Fowler, Sioux Browning, & Denise Ryan. For the complete list of surf spots around Oahu my thanks to Sage Spalding. For another poetry, I thank Chris Haddock & Alan DiFiore. Love & thanks to my mother, to Michael, & to Douglas.

"Apart, I Send You News of Lions" is for Michael Ondaatje
"Aperture" is for Sark Kapena Wetzel
"Canoe" is for Gillian Deacon & Grant Gordon
"Roommate" is for Jane Bohman
"Recipe" is for Kristin Spalding
"Divine" is for Gillian Deacon
"Tadpole Dreams" is for Anne Todgham & Todd Gillis
"The Apprentice" is for Janice Kulyk Keefer
"August, an epilogue" is for Constance Rooke

Jericho, Vancouver 1999